The Best Kind of Kiss

Margaret Allum

illustrated by Jonathan Bentley

Walker & Company New York

For Imogen —M. A.

For Ruby and Harvey —J. B.

3 3113 03047 0241

First published in Australia in 2010 by Little Hare Books, an imprint of Hardie Grant Egmont
Published in the United States of America in December 2011
by Walker Publishing Company, Inc., a division of Bloomsbury Publishing, Inc.
www.bloomsburykids.com

For information about permission to reproduce selections from this book, write to
Permissions, Walker BFYR, 175 Fifth Avenue, New York, New York 10010

Library of Congress Cataloging-in-Publication Data
available upon request
ISBN 978-0-8027-2274-4

Art created with pencil, ink, and wash, with further digital enhancement
Typeset in Shakey Slabserif and WindrowHand Light
Book design by Vida and Luke Kelly

Produced by Pica Digital, Singapore
Printed in China by Phoenix Offset, Shenzhen, Guangdong
1 3 5 7 9 10 8 6 4 2

I like kisses.

I like big kisses

and small kisses,

pecky kisses

and smoochy, lip-smacky kisses.

I kiss the cat for a fluffy kiss

and the dog for a waggly kiss.

I kiss flowers for a petal kiss,

butterflies for a fluttery kiss,

dandelions for a whispery kiss,

and snowflakes
for a frosty kiss.

I kiss after fighting, for a sorry kiss . . .

and after playing,
for a friendly kiss ...

before leaving, for a sad kiss . . .

and when arriving,
for a hello kiss.

I sometimes like a
smelly-yelly-brother kiss.

I often get a rosy-cozy-grandma kiss.

And I always want a
snuggly-cuddly-mommy kiss.

But the best kind of kiss is a
great big bristly-growly-daddy kiss!

That's my favorite kiss of all.